Wallace & Gromit™ ANORAKNOPHOBIA

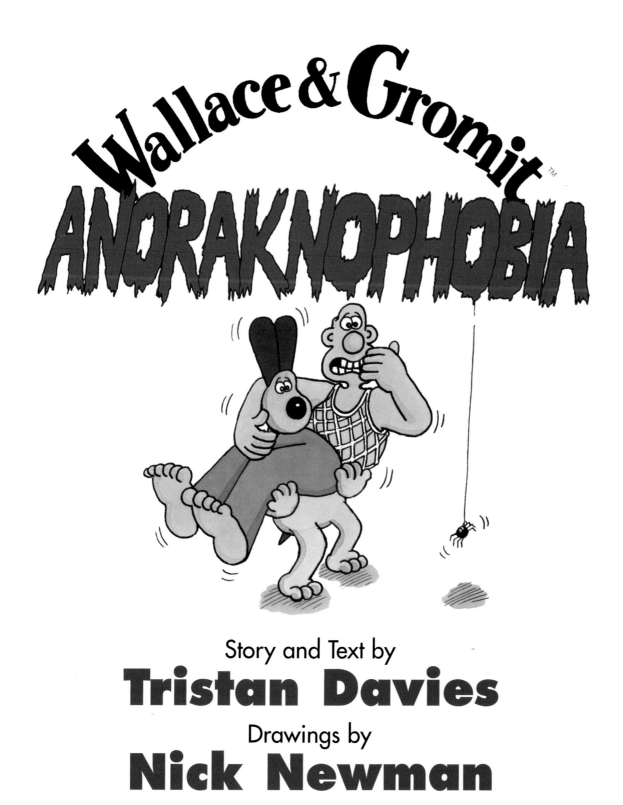

Story and Text by
Tristan Davies
Drawings by
Nick Newman

Hodder & Stoughton

Copyright © 1998 Wallace and Gromit Ltd and Nick Newman and Tristan Davies
based on original characters created by Nick Park Character © and registered trademark
Wallace and Gromit Ltd and Aardman Animations Ltd

Lettering by Gary Gilbert

Additional colouring by
Tony Trimmer and Fiona Newman

First published in Great Britain in 1998 by Hodder & Stoughton
A division of Hodder Headline PLC

The moral rights of Nick Newman and Tristan Davies to be identified as the Authors of the Work have been
asserted by them in accordance with the Copyright, Designs and Patents Act 1988

10 9 8 7 6 5 4 3 2 1

A CIP catalogue record for this title is available from the British Library

ISBN 0 340 71287 2

Printed by Jarrolds Book Printing, Thetford.

Hodder & Stoughton
A division of Hodder Headline PLC
338 Euston Road
London
NW1 3BH

Wallace & Gromit

ANORAKNOPHOBIA

WALLACE

Inventor of the ground- (and furniture) breaking Ping-Pong-O-Matic Automated Home Leisure System who, under hypnosis, learns what it's like to lead a dog's life.

GROMIT

A dog already so busy leading a dog's life (washing the socks, ironing the milk cartons, polishing the Tupperware, etc) he has little time for Home Leisure – even if it is Automated.

MR PATEL

Pigeon fancier and expert on prevailing wind conditions, Wallace's nextdoor neighbour is very interested in, er, wind and pigeons.

DEREK

A game old carrier pigeon and Mr Patel's absolutely favouritest bird.

MR DO IT ALL

Doorman, receptionist, porter, bell boy, gardener and barman at the Hotel Splendio on the Northern Riviera.
(It's a job share.)

THE HERR DOKTOR COUNT BARON NAPOLEON VON STRUDEL, aka BERT MAUDSLEY

Dastardly founder of the Acme Corporation and inventor of the Acme Utility Anorak, he has a surprise up his sleeve and something even yukkier behind his eye patch.

THE CONTESSA BARONESS MADAME FRAULEIN QUEENIE VON STRUDEL, aka QUEENIE MAUDSLEY

Whip-cracking variety artiste whose arachnid trapeze act has mesmerised audiences from Berlin to Barnoldswick – and sometimes all the way back again.

CLEETHORPES and CLITHEROE

Bert and Queenie's polite, erudite twins, whose hobbies are pressing dried flowers and translating the mystical writings of Thomas à Kempis back into Latin.
OR: Two complete and utter nutters. (Delete where applicable.)

DEREK, DERRICK AND ERIC

Gentleman inventors and exhibitionists, who for the purposes of this story are making an exhibition of themselves at an Acme Corporation-sponsored Invention Convention.

THE SPIDERS FROM MARGATE

A troupe of performing arachnids from Margate and the surrounding area (although one, it's true, was brought up by an aunt in Folkestone).

3

4

8

12

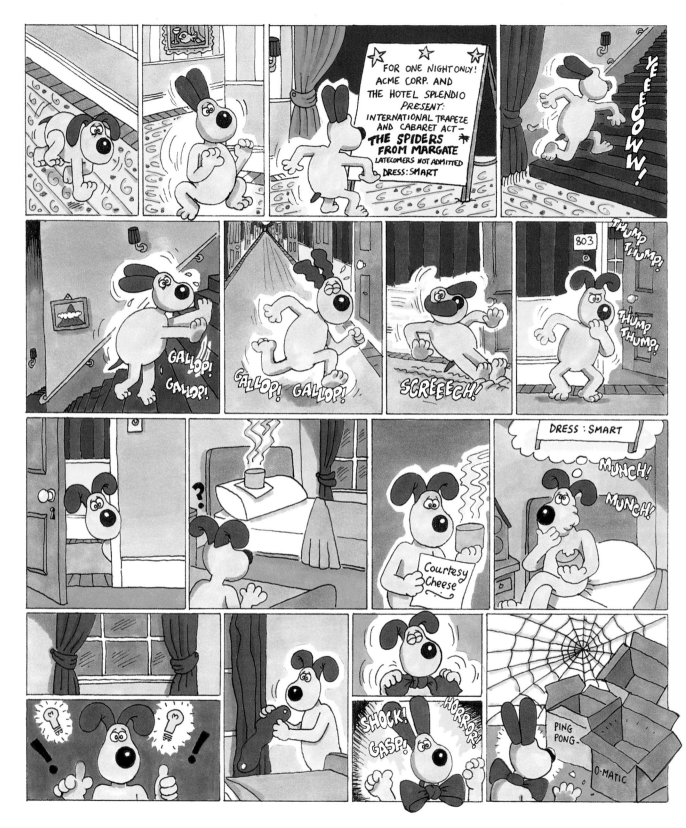

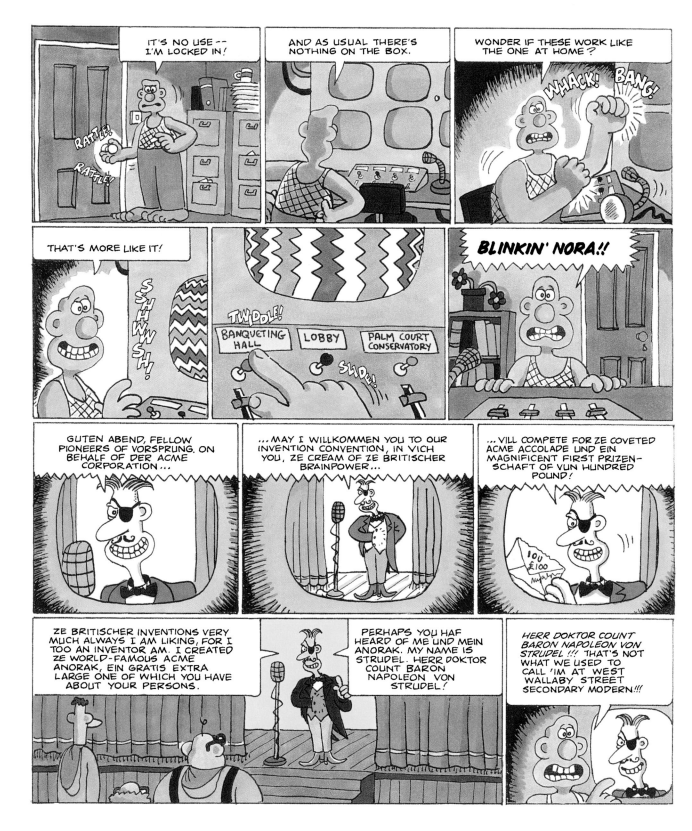

18

21

22

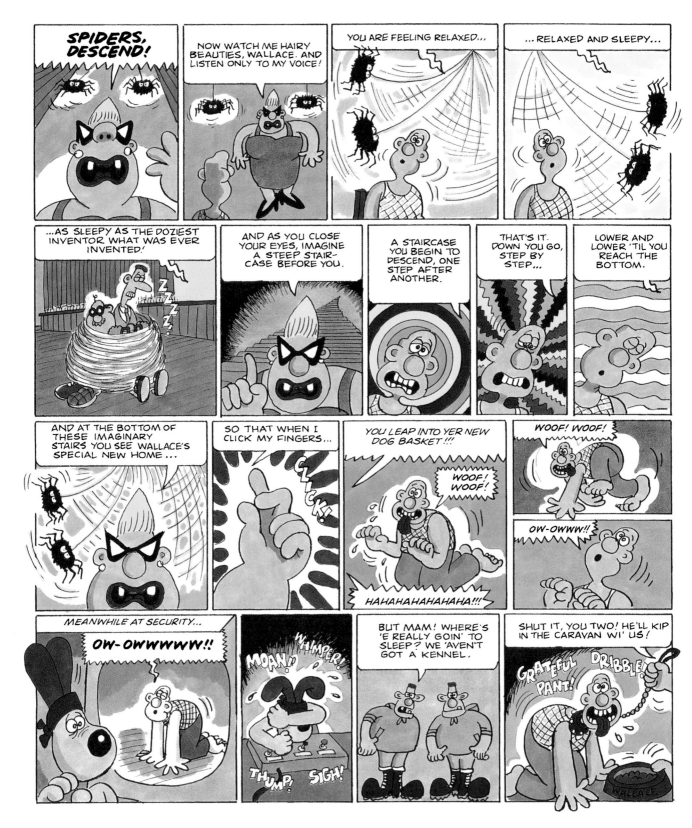

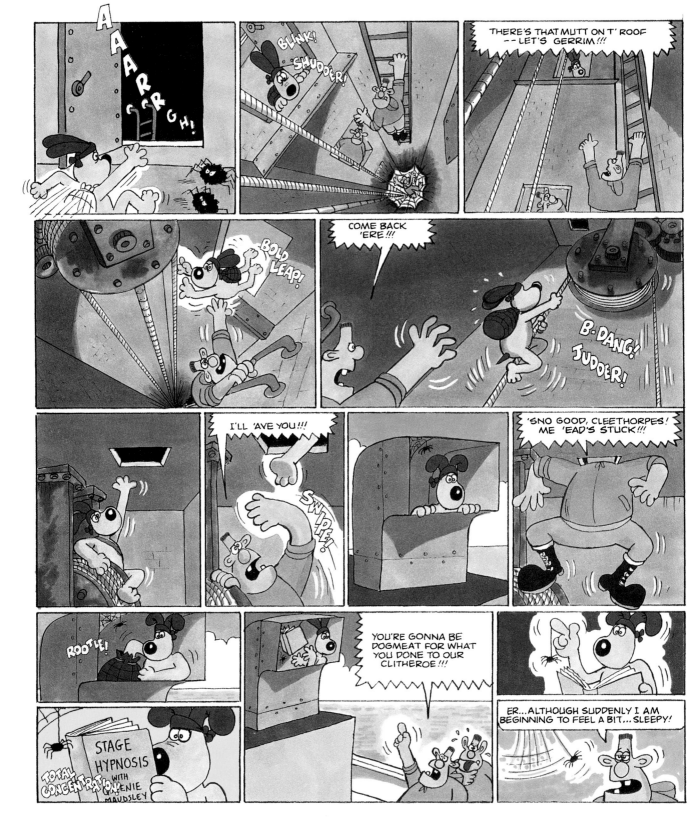

37

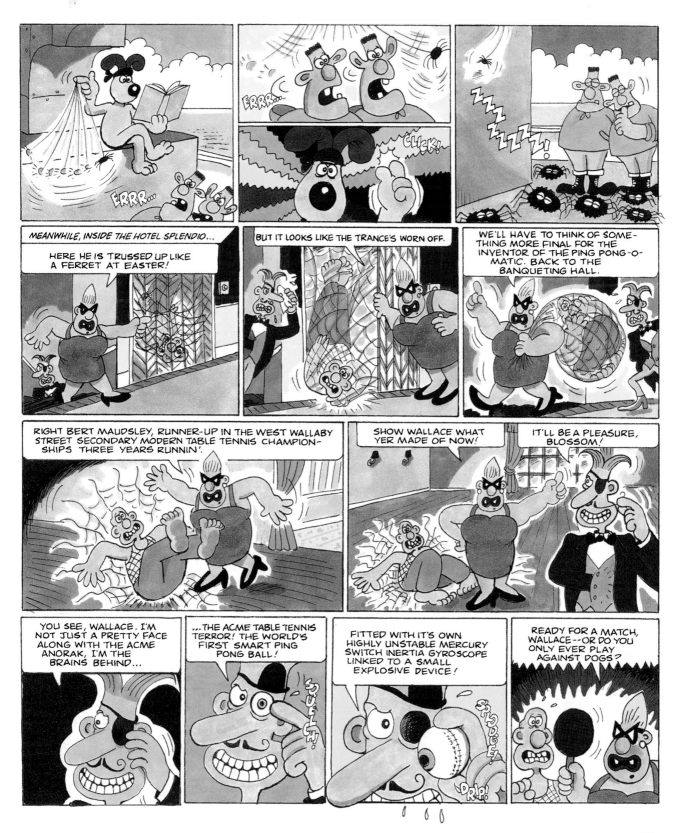

39

40

43

44